R 212
R 220
R 111

For MaryJane.
—E. G. M.

For Braden, Gavin, Elizabeth,
Katelyn, Ashlyne, and Anna—
into the future!
—P. D. G.

This book is for Russell,
who loves to make things
and show them to me.
I hope this book inspires you
as you have inspired me.
—J. G.

 Published simultaneously in Canada. Manufactured in China by South China Printing Co. Ltd. Designed by Gina DiMassi and Julia Gorton. Text set in Antique Olive regular. The art was done in airbrushed acrylic and collage on Strathmore cold press bristol paper. Library of Congress Cataloging-in-Publication Data Hunter, Ryan Ann. Robots slither / by Ryan Ann Hunter; illustrated by Julia Gorton. p. cm. Summary: Rhyming verse describes the many things that robots can do, while sidebars present more detailed information on actual robots today and as planned for the future. [1. Robots—Fiction. 2. Stories in rhyme.] I. Gorton, Julia, ill. II. Title. PZ8.3.H9195 Ro 2004 [E]—dc21 2002031763 ISBN 0-399-23774-7 10 9 8 7 6 5 4 3 2 1 First Impression

ROBOTS SLITHER

by
RYAN ANN HUNTER
illustrated by
JULIA GORTON

G. P. PUTNAM'S SONS
NEW YORK

Robots slither,

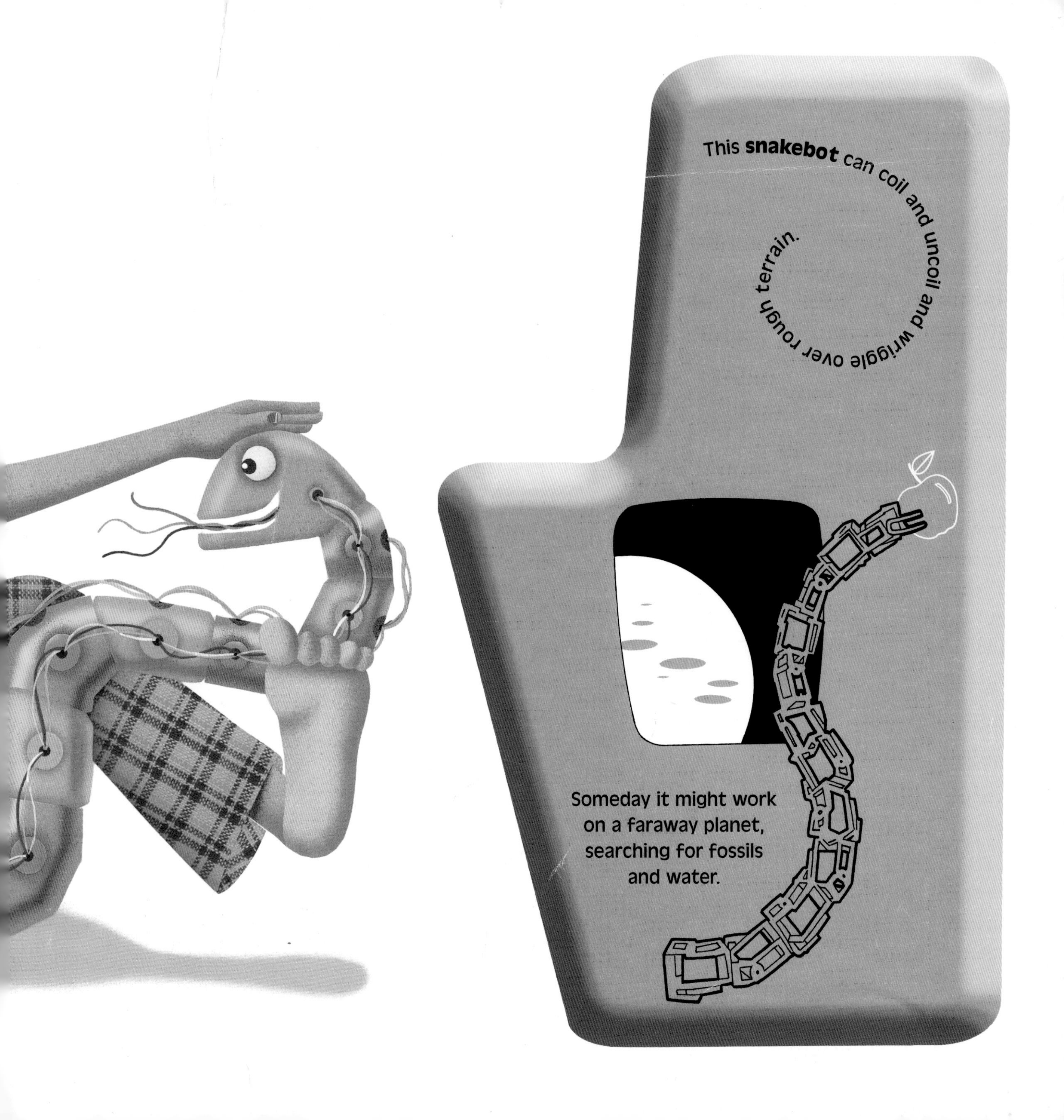

This **snakebot** can coil and uncoil and wriggle over rough terrain.

Someday it might work on a faraway planet, searching for fossils and water.

creep and crawl.

On spiderlike legs, the twelve-foot-high **Dante II** went right into a volcano to test gases there. It dodged rocks that careened down the crater sides.

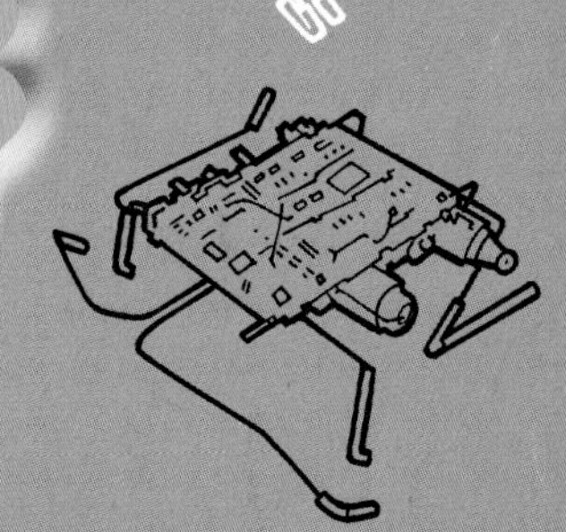

UniBugs are low-tech robots that can poke around on their own. At six or more inches long, they're pretty big bugs!

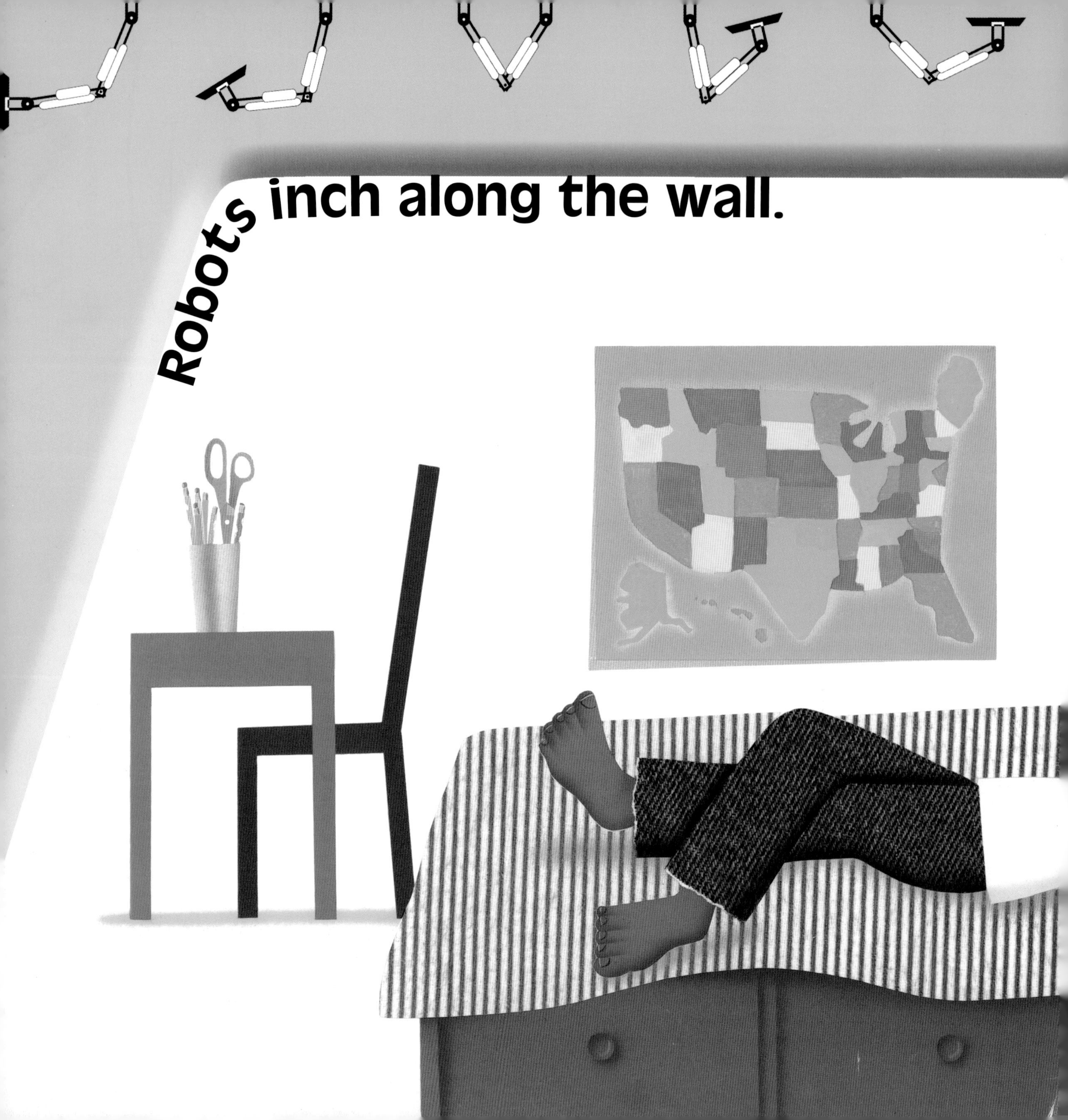

Robots inch along the wall.

This inchworm bot can move on suction-cup feet to snap photos of tiny cracks under a bridge. It could make a good spy!

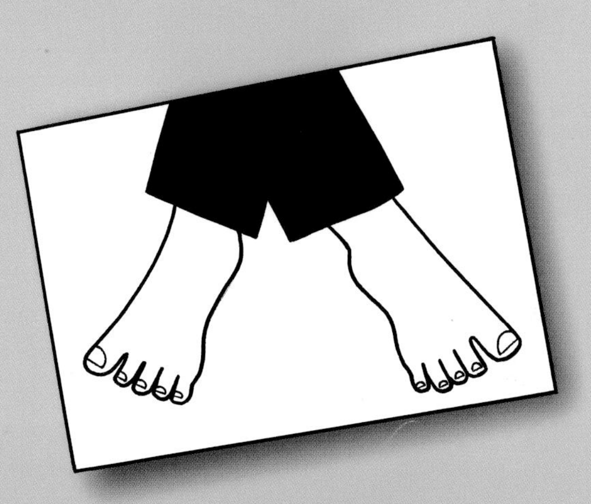

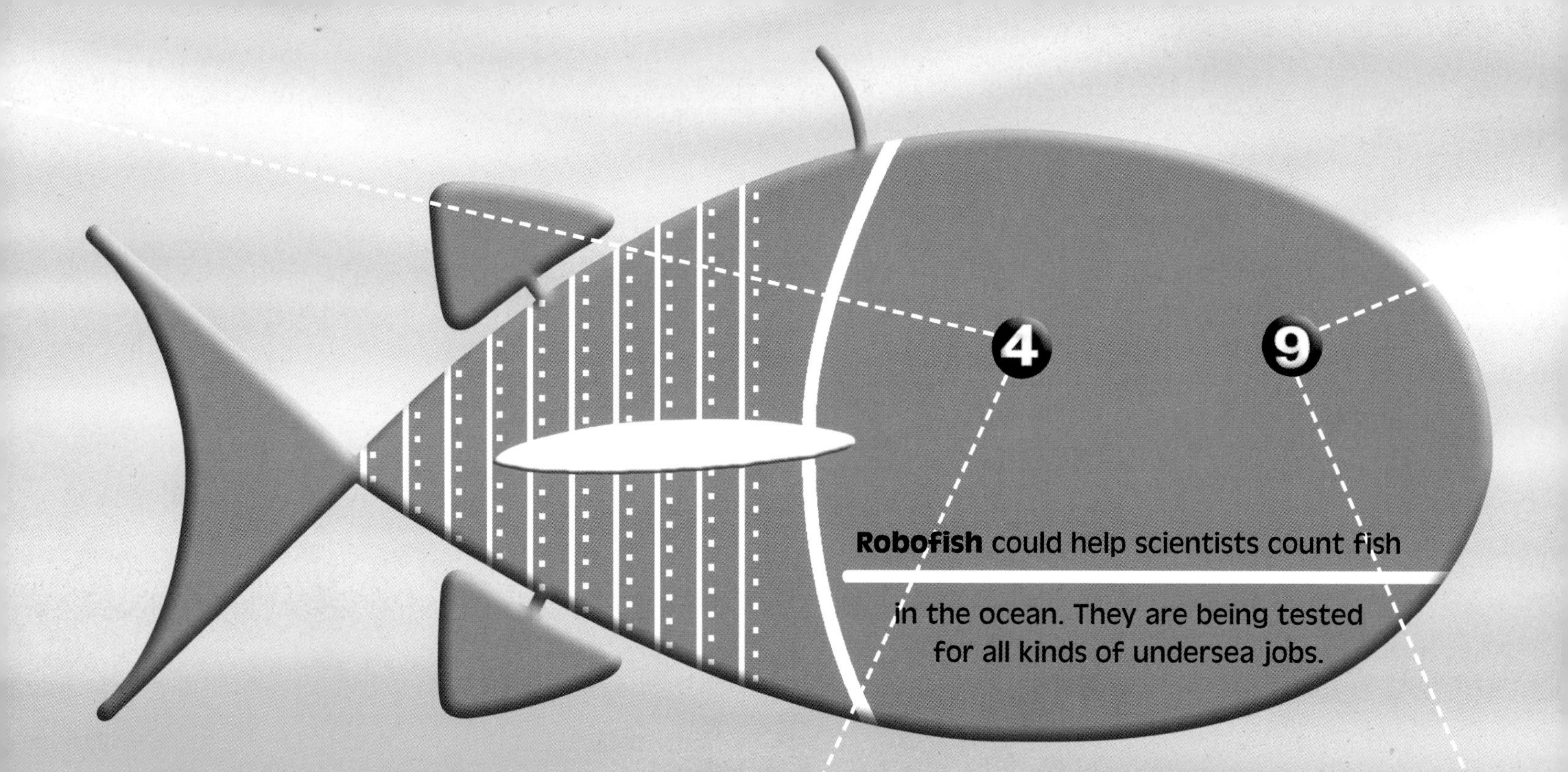

Robofish could help scientists count fish in the ocean. They are being tested for all kinds of undersea jobs.

Robots swim and flick their tails.

Robots dive as deep as whales.

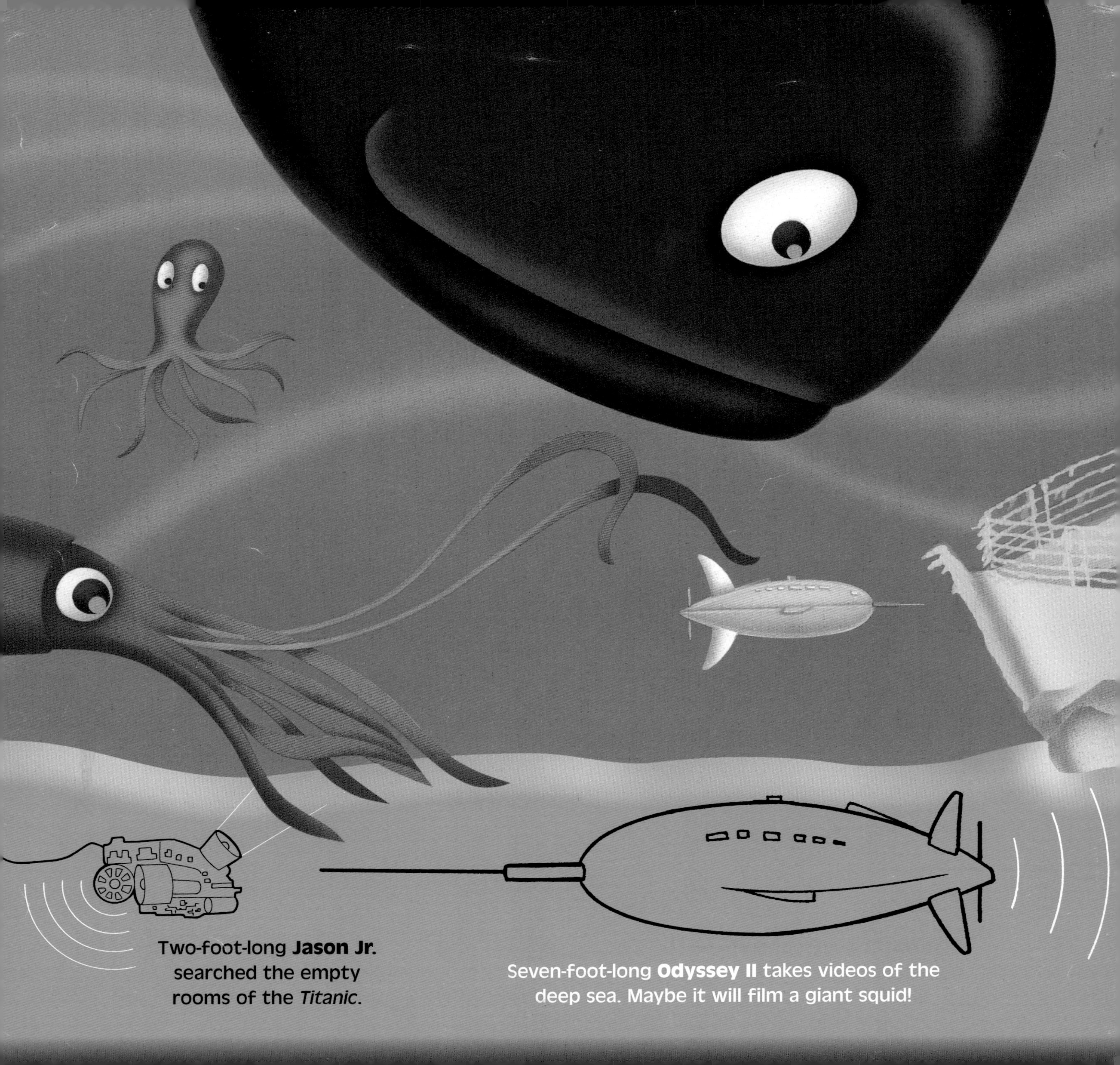

Two-foot-long **Jason Jr.** searched the empty rooms of the *Titanic*.

Seven-foot-long **Odyssey II** takes videos of the deep sea. Maybe it will film a giant squid!

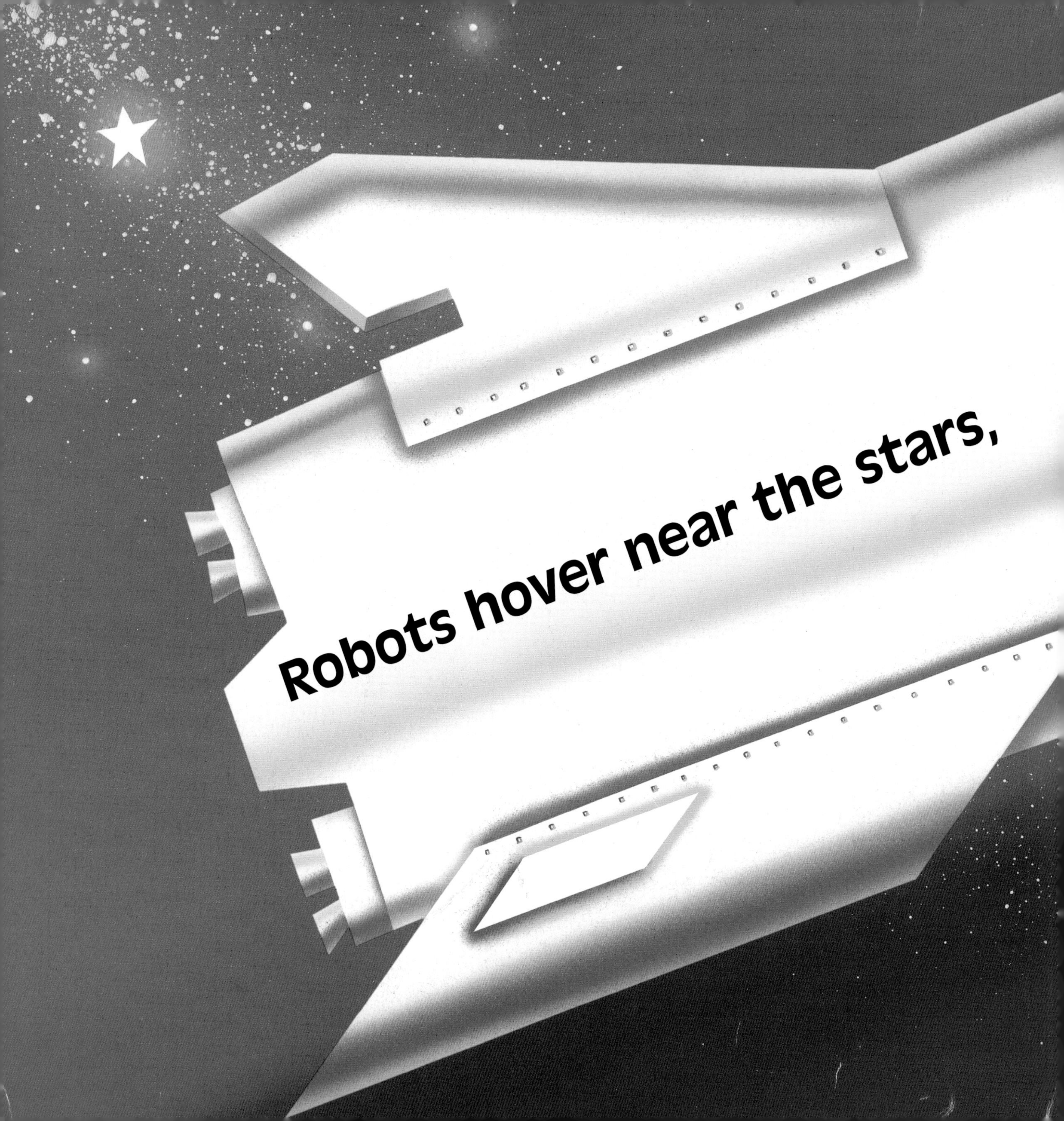

Robots hover near the stars,

PSAs
(Personal Satellite Assistants)
are designed to hang out at the
space station, ready to run errands
for the astronauts. Without gravity
to keep them down, PSAs move
around using small blowers.

hundreds whirring over Mars.

Mesicopters the size of postage stamps could explore Mars. These and other tiny helicopters could keep track of the size and speed of tornadoes and other weather conditions on Earth.

MARS 88

MARS 88

To the rescue robots fly,
zipping, zooming
through the sky.

With infrared cameras, this mini-airplane could find trapped people. Other **MAV**s (Micro Air Vehicles) could monitor traffic, detect poisonous gases and help soldiers stay safe by showing them the location of the enemy.

Robots wheel all about,

Rosie serves lunch to hospital patients. She has a built-in map of the hospital so she knows where to go.
RoboMower cuts the grass. Sensors tell it to stay inside a special wire pegged all around the yard.

Firespy is a
fire-fighting crew
all in one bot!
It runs by itself
or with a driver.

look for danger,
put fires out!

Robots clamp, drill, weld and grip.
On the job, they never slip.

Robots don't get tired of doing the same thing over and over. This robotic arm welds car doors together all day long, day after day.

Minirobots cruise along,
helping fix whatever's wrong.

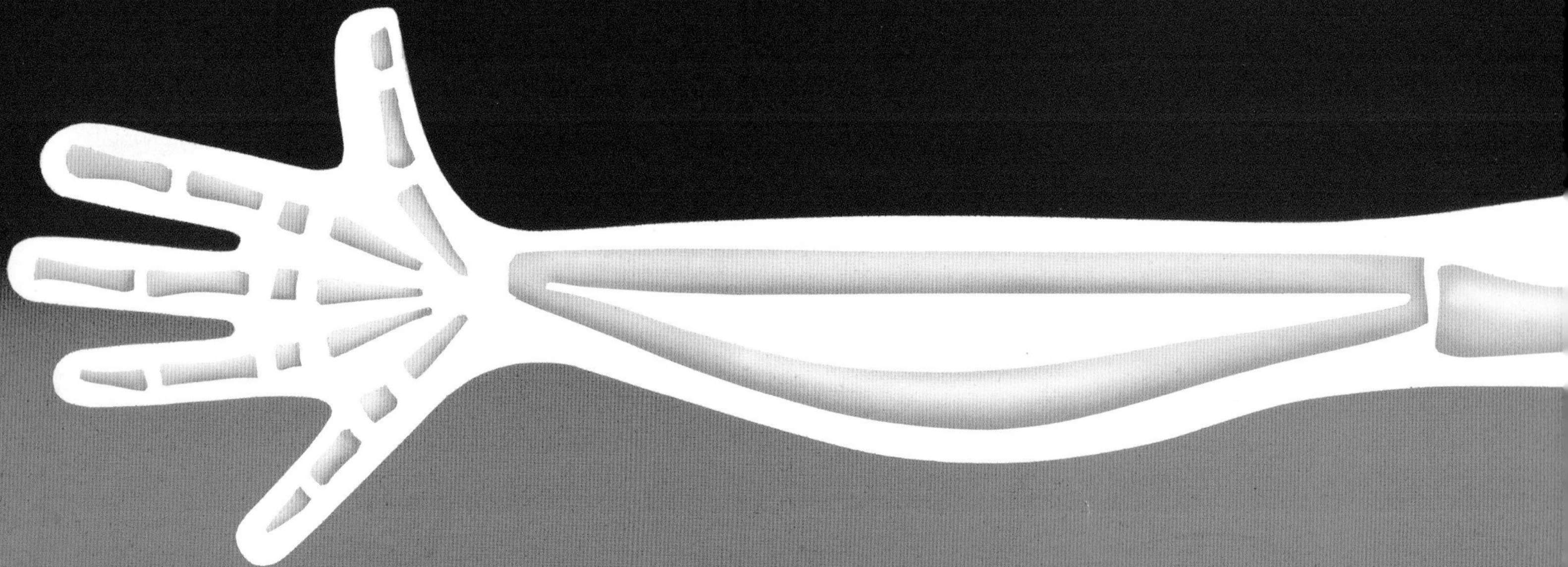

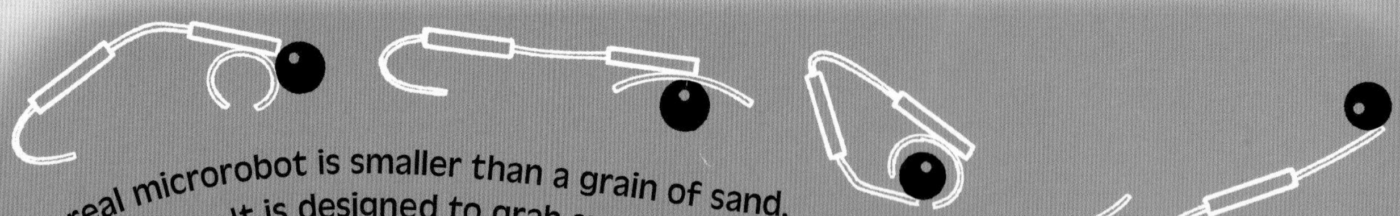

This real microrobot is smaller than a grain of sand.
It is designed to grab super-tiny objects.
Someday robots may be able to travel in
your bloodstream to bring medicine and help repair cells.

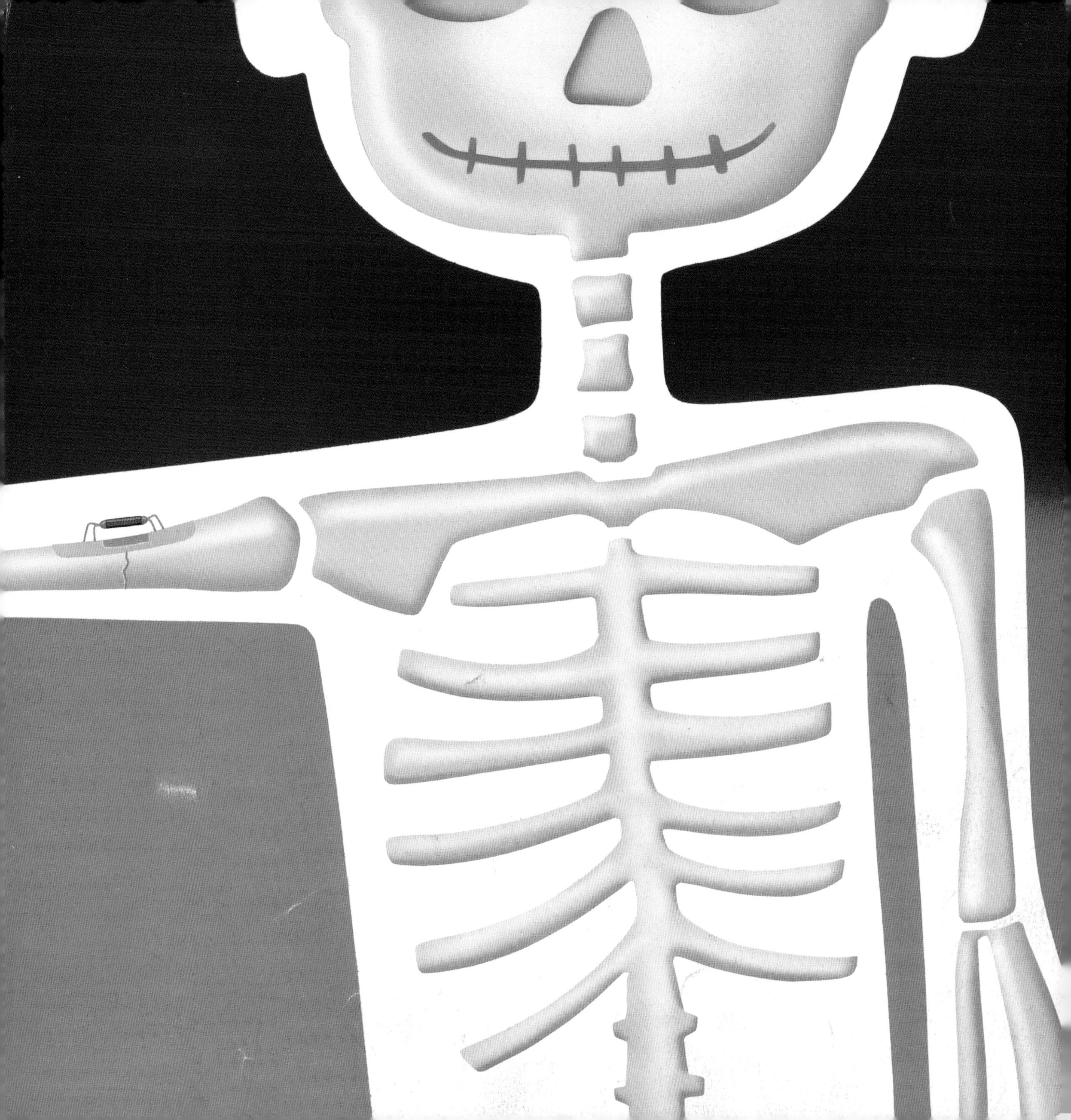

**Troody struts across the floor,
the first robot dinosaur.**

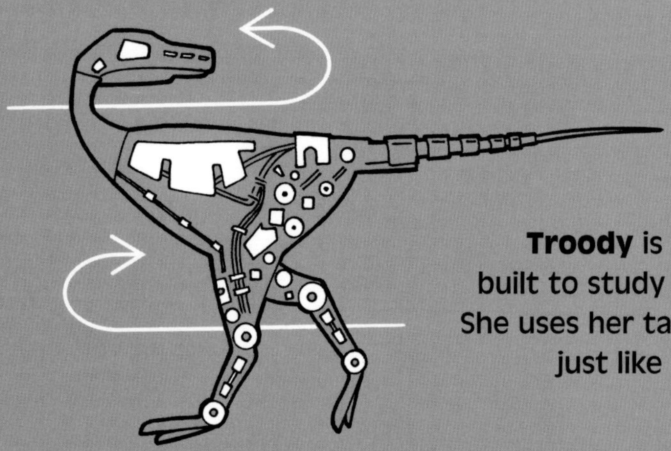

Troody is a life-sized model
built to study dinosaur movement.
She uses her tail to balance and turn,
just like a real Troodon.

Robots shake your hand and talk,
open doors, go for a walk.

Asimo can do many humanlike things. Someday it may be a home helper.

Robopuppies bark "Bow-wow!"
Robokittens say "Meow!"

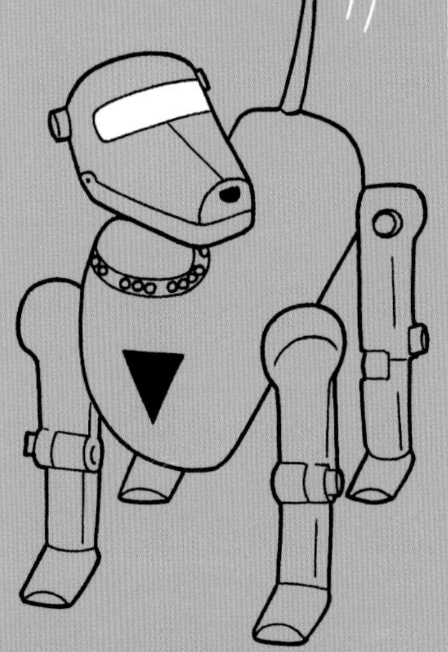

Robot pets know their names and follow lots of commands. They don't need to be housebroken!

Look at what these robots do— smile at them, they'll smile at you!

Kismet was built so robots can learn to tell what we're feeling by our facial expressions.

ROBONOTE

A few hundred years ago, clock makers adapted the way clocks work to make toys that could repeat movements. Life-sized mechanical dolls played pianos, drew pictures, and wrote notes. Mechanical birds flapped their wings and sang.

People dreamed about having humanlike machines that could also do work, not just entertain. The name robot came from the Czech word *robota* which means having to do work for others.

In the 1950s, engineers designed the first robots to work in factories. They were just steel arms with hands that could be clamps or claws, suction pads or magnets.

Getting robots to move from place to place was the next step. First they got around on wheels. But it took a long time to figure out how to get a robot to balance on two legs. Now robots slither, crawl, swim, fly, hop, and walk!

Today's robots have computers for brains. They run on batteries, electricity, and even solar power. To figure out what's around them, they use sensors like we use eyes, ears, and noses. Scientists are working on artificial intelligence, trying to get robots to think for themselves. So far, robots only have brain power equal to that of insects. We have a long way to go to understand the workings of the human brain.

ROBOSITES

www.idahoptv.org/dialogue4kids/robotics
www.thetech.org/hyper/robots
www.androidworld.com
robotics.jpl.nasa.gov
www.asimo.honda.com

The authors thank those who provided technical information and reference material.

Page 6-7: Snakebot, NASA Ames Research Center. **Page 8-9**: Dante II, Robotics Institute, Carnegie Mellon University; UniBug, BEAM Online. **Page 10-11**: Inchworm robot, Intelligent Robotics Laboratory, Vanderbilt University. **Page 12-13**: Robofish, MIT Sea Grant College Program. **Page 14-15**: Odyssey II, MIT Sea Grant AUV Laboratory; Jason Jr., Woods Hole Oceanographic Institution. **Page 16-17**: PSA, NASA Ames Research Center. **Page 18-19**: Mesicopter, Aircraft Aerodynamics and Design Group, Stanford University. **Page 20-21**: Mini-airplane, MIT Lincoln Laboratory. **Page 22-23**: HelpMate, Cardinal Health, Pyxis Products and Services; RoboMower, Friendly Robotics. **Page 24-25**: Firespy, JCB Inc. **Page 26-27**: Robotic arm, Getty Images. **Page 28-29**: Microrobot, Edwin Jager, Linköpings Universitet & Micromuscle AB. **Page 30-31**: Troody, Dinosaur Robots, Inc. **Page 32-33**: Asimo Humanoid Robot, American Honda Motor Company, Inc. **Page 34-35**: RS-01, RoboScience Ltd. **Page 36-37**: Kismet, MIT Artificial Intelligence Laboratory.